AF552346

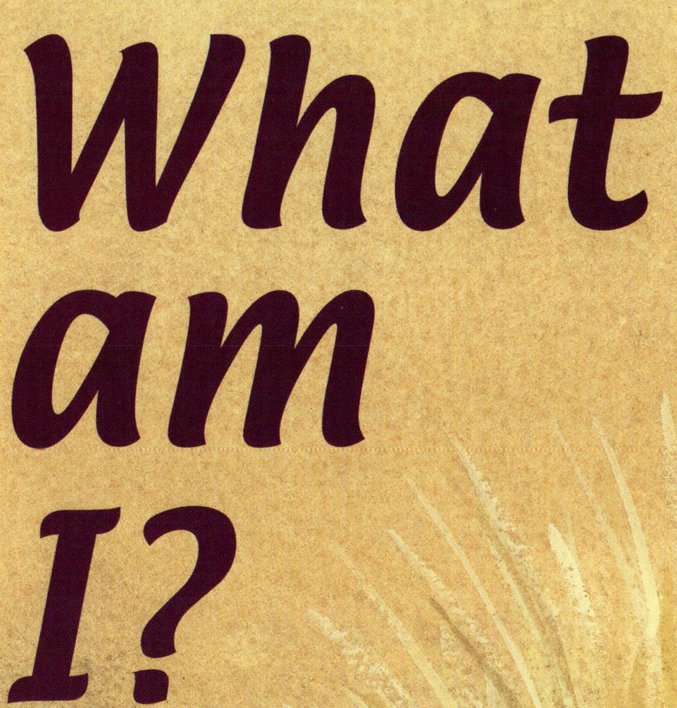

Kim Dale

I bat my lovely lashes
over big brown eyes.
My body is feathered,
I'm quite a size.
My legs are long,
I run with grace,
But my very best feature
Is my beautiful face.

What am I?

I am an emu.

In black and white, my coat is trim.
On land I'm slow, but when I swim
I fly on wings,
Swift and sleek,
Catching fish with my beak.
I am the fairy of the sea.
Now that's a clue —
Can you name me?

What am I?

I am a fairy penguin.

I'm red or grey.
My tail is long.
My legs are specially
Big and strong
So I can run
And leap with ease.
I have a pouch.
What am I, please?

What am I?

I am a kangaroo.

You'll find me underwater
In a quiet stream or creek.
I have a pouch, yet I lay eggs.
I also have webbed feet.
Some say my bill is like a duck's.
I'm shiny brown and sleek.
I'm very shy, so quiet, please,
If you want to take a peek.

What am I?

I am a platypus.

Don't get a fright
If you see me at night.
I'm fat and friendly as can be.
I make my burrow underground,
And after dark I roam around
To find my food.
Can you see me?

What am I?

I am a wombat.

Though my spines are sharp
I'm very shy.
So please be quiet
As I pass by.
I create a kerfuffle
When I burrow and snuffle
To find juicy ants —
Then off I shuffle.

What am I?

I am an echidna.

My fur is grey.
My nose is black.
I carry my babies
On my back.
I sleep all day.
I live in trees.
I rarely drink,
And I eat gum leaves.

What am I?

I am a koala.

When predators try to eat me
They may think I'm quite a prize.
But I quickly turn and face them,
And I'm suddenly twice my size.
For I'm the frill-necked lizard!
I will not hide from you —
I'll stand up tall, frilled-neck held high,
And look you boldly in the eye!

I'm a fine feathered fellow,
As happy as can be.
I sit all day and cackle
In the old gum tree.
Listen very carefully
By the billabong,
Whoo, whoo, whoo, ha, ha, ha
Is my merry song.

What am I?

I am a kookaburra.

I'm crisp black and white.
I'm cheeky and strong.
I'm the sound of the dawn
With my carolling song.
With my beautiful music
I make the bush ring,
But don't come too close
To my nest-tree in spring!

What am I?

I am a magpie.

Maybe I came
From Asia long ago,
But now I'm Australian,
I hunt high and low.
The difference between
A domestic dog and me
Is a howl but no bark.
So what could I be?

What am I?

I am a dingo.
This is my family.

I have a long and curling tail.
My fur is soft and grey.
I live in trees and feed at night,
I sleep throughout the day.
When at dusk I quietly leave
My snuggly tree-trunk nook,
Shyly I sneak, stop and peek,
With bulging eyes I look.

What am I?

I am a ringtail possum.

You'll often find me basking
In the morning sun,
To warm my scaly body,
When the day has just begun.
I flick my long forked tongue
To check scents in the breeze.
I'm powerful and agile —
I run and climb up trees.

What am I?

I am a goanna.

I'm called a devil —
Now, there's a clue.
I'm small, black and fierce,
Though no threat to you.
I use my powerful jaws and claws
To crunch up all my prey,
And having roamed to feed all night,
I go to sleep all day.

What am I?

I am a Tasmanian devil.

FAUNA FACTS

A NOTE ON MAMMALS

There are three types of mammals:

Placental mammals

Placental mammals have a long pregnancy during which the embryo is nourished through the placenta. The young are born well developed and continue to feed on milk. Humans, whales and bats are placental mammals.

Marsupials

These pouched mammals have a short pregnancy; then the young continue to develop over a long period in the pouch, feeding on milk. Kangaroos, possums, koalas and wombats are marsupials.

Monotremes

Monotremes lay eggs and, when the young hatch, they feed on milk. There are only three monotremes in the world — the platypus, the Australian echidna and the New Guinea echidna.

EMU

Dromaius novaehollandiae

Emus lead a nomadic existence throughout southern Australia. They stand 2 m tall and weigh up to 45 kg. Although they do not fly, they are capable of running very fast and can move over vast distances in search of food.

They live on flowers, seeds, fruits, young shoots and insects, leaving an area only when the food supply is exhausted. The male emu incubates the eggs and raises the brood of young chicks without help from the female.

LITTLE PENGUIN OR FAIRY PENGUIN

Eudyptula minor

The fairy penguin has an average length of 40 cm and weighs between 1 and 2 kg. These flightless birds are found in colonies along the southern coast of Australia.

The most aquatic of all birds, penguins are supreme swimmers. Using their wings for propulsion, they actually 'fly' underwater, with their tails serving as rudders. They feed on fish, squid and other small invertebrates, which they eat underwater.

Fairy penguins lay two eggs in a nest under rocks or in dense undergrowth or in a burrow in soft sand. The eggs hatch in five weeks. For another seven weeks the parent birds take turns in guarding the chicks and fishing to feed them.

At Phillip Island in Victoria, thousands of tourists delight in watching the penguins parade up the beach at dusk, on their way back to their burrows.

EASTERN GREY KANGAROO

Macropus giganteus

The mature male kangaroo stands approximately 2 m tall and weighs as much as 70 kg. Kangaroos' habitats range from semi-arid scrub to woodlands and forests. They are mainly grazing animals, preferring grass, which they eat from dusk to dawn. Eastern grey kangaroos are distributed throughout eastern Australia, including Tasmania.

Kangaroos have extremely strong hind legs that enable them to hop at very fast speeds, using their tails for balance.

The female gives birth to a tiny joey, only 2 cm long. It finds its way into the pouch, attaching itself to one of two teats. It feeds on milk for eleven months, then leaves the pouch but still suckles while grazing for another seven months. A new joey will be in the pouch by then. The mother produces different milk for each joey.

PLATYPUS

Ornithorhynchus anatinus

The platypus is unique — an amphibious monotreme which lays eggs, has a bill and webbed feet like a duck, and suckles its young.

Platypuses weigh approximately 2 kg and are about 50 cm long. They are commonly distributed in freshwater rivers, streams and lakes in eastern Australia. Active at night, they locate food such as insects, larvae, worms, frogs and crustaceans, using their duck-like bills, which contain nerve receptors that are sensitive to the tiny electrical fields around moving things. They store food in a cheek pouch and go to the water surface to chew. Thick fur keeps them dry and warm.

When out of water, platypuses live in burrows dug into the side of a stream. In a nesting chamber in the burrow the female lays one to three eggs (most commonly one), which hatch after ten days. Although she feeds her babies on milk, the female has no nipples. Instead, the milk oozes onto her fur, which the baby licks and sucks.

At four months the young leave the burrow. Then at six months they go off alone to find their own territory.

COMMON WOMBAT

Vombatus ursinus

This large burrowing marsupial, found mainly in south-eastern Australia, averages 1 m in length and weighs approximately 30 kg. Its habitat varies from grasslands and mountainous areas to coastal forest. Mainly nocturnal, wombats feed on native grasses, roots, leaves and sedges. With their powerful limbs they dig burrows up to 20 m long, which branch into several chambers.

The newborn starts life the size of a bean, finding its way into a backward-facing pouch (so the pouch isn't filled with dirt). It spends the next six months in the pouch, attached to a teat. After leaving the pouch, the cub spends a further twelve months with its mother.

Although wombats show little fear of humans, be careful not to block their path — these Aussie bulldozers are known for sudden bursts of speed and they can bowl you over and bite.

ECHIDNA

Tachyglossus aculeatus

The short-beaked echidna is a monotreme and the only native mammal found throughout Australia, from deserts to snow-covered mountains. Echidnas living in cold climates have hair between their spines for warmth, which almost hides their spines.

Echidnas weigh between 2 and 7 kg and are 30–45 cm long. Their diet is ants and termites, which they collect on their long, sticky tongues, which can move in all directions and flicker in and out about 100 times a minute. Echidnas have the amazing ability to sink below the surface of the soil without moving backwards or forwards. To defend themselves, they roll into a ball of spines or wedge themselves forcefully against rocks or logs, making them difficult to budge.

The female echidna lays one soft-skinned egg which she claws into her pouch. Ten days later the egg hatches and the baby, known as a 'puggle', will stay in the pouch feeding on milk until its spines start growing. When this becomes uncomfortable for the mother, she claws the puggle out and places it on a nest in a burrow. At six months the young echidna leaves the burrow, staying with its mother for another four weeks.

KOALA

Phascolarctos cinereus

The koala is distributed throughout eastern Australia. It averages 75 cm in length and weighs approximately 10 kg. It feeds predominantly on the leaves of eucalypts (gum trees) and, because these gum leaves are high in water content, koalas normally do not need to drink. They sleep in the forks of trees for most of the day. They are accomplished climbers and move about quickly just after sunset.

Like wombats and echidnas, koalas have backward-facing pouches. At birth, the young koala finds its way into the pouch and attaches itself to a teat. It feeds on milk for six months. After leaving the pouch, the young koala travels on its mother's back, feeding on both milk and eucalyptus leaves until it is a year old.

In the past it was thought koalas were drowsy because of a drug in eucalyptus leaves. This is not so. The gum leaves have very few nutrients and are hard to digest, so the koala needs to move slowly and rest a lot to conserve energy for when it is needed most.

FRILL-NECKED LIZARD

Chlamydosaurus kingii

One of Australia's most famous reptiles, the frill-necked lizard is found in open scrub country, spending most of its time in trees hunting insects.

It can move very quickly and runs on its hind legs. When alarmed, the lizard raises its frill by opening its mouth wide and hisses loudly. It is capable of inflicting nasty wounds with its sharp teeth. Its average length is 75 cm.

KOOKABURRA

Dacelo novaeguineae

The kookaburra is Australia's best-known bird, with its distinctive laughing cry. Although it is a large kingfisher, it lives on insects, small animals and reptiles. Its habitat is forests and eucalypt woodlands throughout eastern Australia.

Kookaburras live for twenty years and have one mate for life. They usually nest in tree holes, where the female sits on a clutch of eggs for three to four weeks. Five weeks later, the fledglings leave the nest, but the parents continue to feed them for a further two to three months. The young birds from past seasons stay with the parents for four or five years, helping with parenting the younger birds and also to ensure the family's hold on the territory.

AUSTRALIAN MAGPIE

Gymnorhina tibicen

The Australian magpie is well known for its melodious song, which can be heard both in the bush and in the suburbs, all over most of Australia. No relation to the European magpie, it is closely related to butcherbirds and currawongs. Its diet consists mainly of insects, invertebrates and sometimes small lizards and mice, and it spends a lot of time feeding on the ground.

Always willing to accept a meal, this delightful bird can become quite tame and will often take food from your hand. It helps if you befriend your local magpies, especially during nesting time, when they are well known for swooping at strangers who come too close to the nesting tree. The parent birds are concerned and want the area clear of danger when their fledglings leave the nest. At this stage the fledglings can not fly very well and are vulnerable to predators.

DINGO

Canis familiaris dingo

The dingo is a primitive dog, not native to Australia. It differs from the domestic dog in that it breeds only once a year (domestic dogs can breed twice yearly), and it has no bark.

It is thought that dingos were introduced by the Australian Aborigines thousands of years ago. Dingoes are found throughout mainland Australia, although they are becoming rare in the eastern states.

Dingos hunt singly or in family groups. Their diet consists mainly of mammals, but they also eat some reptiles and birds.

Female dingos give birth to an average of five pups, but a litter can be any number up to ten. The pups are reared in a den and weaned at five months.

COMMON RINGTAIL POSSUM

Pseudocheirus peregrinus

Ringtail possums have adapted to living in cities and towns, as well as in their bush habitat. These shy, furry, nocturnal mammals feed mainly on leaves, fruit and flowers. Using their strong, sharp claws for climbing and their long ringtails for holding onto branches, they spend most of their time in trees.

Ringtails grow to the size of a small cat. The female has one to four young, which she carries and suckles in her pouch for up to four months. When the young are old enough to leave the pouch, she will care for them as they cling to her back.

During the day the common ringtail rests in a nest called a 'drey'. Built in tree hollows or dense undergrowth, the drey is about the size of a football and lined with shredded bark and grasses.

GOANNA OR YELLOW-SPOTTED MONITOR

Varanus panoptes

Of the thirty-four species of monitors in the world, twenty-five are found in the arid or tropical regions of Australia.

The goanna or yellow-spotted monitor is approximately 1.5 m long and has powerful limbs that enable it to run and climb with speed and agility. Its tail is unusually long and provides support when the goanna stands on its hind legs. The tail is also used as a weapon to lash out at a predator. Goannas flick their forked tongues in and out to pick up scents. Goannas do not eat vegetable matter. They hunt lizards, snakes, birds, mammals, insects and frogs.

TASMANIAN DEVIL

Sarcophilus harrisii

The Tasmanian devil is a carnivorous marsupial whose eerie, whining screams are partly responsible for its name. Short and heavy-set, with a large head and powerful legs, it is found throughout Tasmania, but is more common in the north. Tasmanian devils disappeared from the Australian mainland when the dingo arrived.

This solitary animal feeds at night, preferring carrion (dead meat). With powerful jaws and sharp teeth, it eats every part of the animal, including the skull. They are able to climb trees and will sometimes catch birds. During the day they rest in hollow logs and caves.

The females carry up to four young in a backward-facing pouch for about five months. Then the young stay in a den with the mother for another six months.

Acknowledgement
To my family, those who came into my life at the right time freely offering their knowledge and, most of all, to the injured and sick wildlife I have cared for who taught me so much

REFERENCES

The Australian Wildlife Year, Reader's Digest, Sydney, 1989

Reader's Digest Encyclopaedia of Wildlife, Reader's Digest, Sydney, 1997

Strahan, Ronald (ed.), *The Australian Museum Complete Book of Australian Mammals*, Angus & Robertson, Sydney, 1983

Wilson, Steven K. & David G. Knowles, *Australia's Reptiles, a Photographic Reference to Terrestrial Reptiles of Australia*, Collins, Sydney, 1998

Thomas C. Lothian Pty Ltd
11 Munro Street, Port Melbourne, Victoria 3207

First published 1999

National Library of Australia
Cataloguing-in-Publication data:

Dale, Kim.
What am I?

ISBN 07344 0044 6.

1. Animals – Australia – Juvenile literature. 2. Games.

591.991

Colour reproduction by Color Gallery, Kuala Lumpur
Printed in Hong Kong by South China Printing